Maddie in Danger

Louise Leblanc

Illustrations by Marie-Louise Gay

Translated by Sarah Cummins

Formac Publishing
Halifax, Nova Scotia
1995

Canadian Cataloguing in Publication Data

Leblanc, Louise, 1942-

  [Sophie est en danger. English]

  Maddie in danger

  (First Novel Series)

  Translation of: Sophie est en danger.

ISBN 0-88780-306-7 (paper)
ISBN 0-88780-307-5 (board)

I. Gay, Marie-Louise. II. Title. III. Title: Sophie est en danger. English. IV. Series.

PS8573.E25S6413   1995   j843'.54   C95-950088-X
P27.L42Ma 1995

Formac Publishing Limited
5502 Atlantic Street
Halifax, N.S. B3H 1G4

Printed and bound in Canada

Table of contents

Chapter 1
The Screaming Shooter   5

Chapter 2
A Trip to the Video Store   15

Chapter 3
Very Scary   23

Chapter 4
A Talk with Gran   29

Chapter 5
A Triumph for Maddie, but ...   37

Chapter 6
Maddie versus the Exterminator   45

Chapter 7
Maddie, Leader of the Gang   55

1
The Screaming Shooter

My parents are going on a trip. They need to get away. They keep bugging Alexander and me, even though we are getting along better than we ever have.

Yesterday we invited all our friends over, and then it started to rain. So we organized a treasure hunt in the house.

Nobody was fighting or anything, but my mother was really hyper. Today she told us our friends could not come over again. She said she is counting on us to help her before she goes.

My father was more specific

"You two will watch your little sister while we pack. And no mischief!"

Grrr! What kind of mischief can you get into with a two-year-old baby? Anyway, Angelbaby was sleeping. The worst that could happen was if she had a nightmare.

Alexander went over and picked up the gun he had hidden behind the sofa.

"See, you lift this handle, and then you push this button, and it starts," he explained.

"Hoyyhayaarghhueuurha..."

Wow! It sounded just like someone writhing in pain.

I grabbed the gun for my turn and shot. It let out a terrible cry of suffering: "RRRAAAAAAAAAR-GAAAAA".

Angelbaby woke up and started to cry while I was shooting at Alexander. He screamed and dropped to the ground.

My parents ran in. They must have thought Angelbaby had hurt herself because they started examining her all over.

When they saw she was all right, they turned around and saw the gun and Alexander, sprawled out on the floor. Like an idiot, he was playing dead.

Instantly, my parents turned totally white. If they'd been any whiter, they would have been phosphorescent.

Just then my brother Julian walked in. He looked around at everyone and said in a fury, "You're playing the Exterminator without me! That's not nice.

I want to play the Exterminator too!"

He grabbed the gun, put his glasses back on his nose, and fired on the entire family. A hail of groans burst out of the gun.

Alexander was still dead, and a good thing too, for him, because my dad was getting angry. If he'd turned any redder, he would have exploded. In fact, he did explode.

"WHAT IS THAT THING?"

"It's the Exterminator's Screaming Shooter. The Exterminator is a really bad guy who wants to exterminate everyone in his movie," answered Julian.

My dad did not seem satisfied with this response.

"MADDIE! WHERE DID THIS GUN COME FROM?"

"I don't know. Alexander—"

"ALEXANDER!" bellowed my father.

I think that right then Alexander did actually die of fright, because he didn't move a muscle.

"Alexander," said my mother calmly, "will you kindly resuscitate yourself immediately and tell us about this gun?"

Alexander returned to the living, but he still looked kind of dead.

"It belongs to a friend of mine," he mumbled. "I told him that we didn't have a Screaming Shooter at our house, and he couldn't believe it! He let me borrow his, so at least we would know what it was."

I thought this would be a good

time to transmit a little message to my parents.

"All our friends think we are absolute idiots, because they watch all the latest shows and we don't. This evening, they're all going to watch *The Exterminator* on television."

"You are definitely not allowed to watch that kind of film," my mother declared immediately.

I can't believe it! My parents have never seen this film, and yet they act like they know all about it. They make all these decisions for us, without even knowing what they're talking about. I told them so.

"We are well aware that *The Exterminator* is an extremely violent film that could MARK

YOU FOR LIFE," my mother cut me off. "That's all we need to know."

"Anyway, *The Exterminator* is a bomb," added my father.

"No, he isn't, Dad," Julian piped up, totally out of it. "He's an extraterrestrial."

"I meant that the film *The Exterminator* is a bomb, it stinks, it's no good."

"I know he's not GOOD!" Julian cried. "He slices up people with his gun and makes them into sandwiches. Like this!"

Julian demonstrated by shooting the gun at Angelbaby, who began to scream as loud as the shooter.

My dad screamed even louder, just to make himself heard.

"ENOUGH!"

Everything stopped screaming. In a voice like steel, my father said, "I never again want to hear *The Exterminator* mentioned in this house. Is that clear?"

Grrr! Why do we have to have such strict parents? They won't let us develop like normal kids. Maybe we can catch up while they're away...

2
A Trip to the Video Store

My parents told us a million things to do and not to do while they were away. Then a million more for Gran, who was looking after us. As soon as they left, everyone forgot everything they had said.

Gran did not put Angelbaby down for her nap the way my mom told her to. Instead she started playing with her and giggling. And she let Julian watch television.

I asked her if I could go to the Garcia's corner store with Alexander. It's just down the street.

She said we could go and gave us a little wink.

"Just don't eat too much candy!"

When we were alone, I said to Alexander, "Poor Gran. She actually thinks we eat candy in secret."

"Yeah," laughed Alexander. "She doesn't realize we like chips now."

Honestly, what a nerd. I wondered if he might be too young to take part in my plan. On the other hand, I needed his help.

"I hope you brought your money? We need it for my plan."

"A plan? For buying chips? No way! You buy your chips, I'll buy mine."

Grrr! I tell you, it takes a lot of

patience to get what you want.
Fortunately, I am a very patient
person.

"Not for buying chips, idiot!
A plan for *The Exterminator*."

"The film? But it was on TV

last night..."

"We have a VCR! And the video store is right next door to the corner store, so..."

"You want to rent the video? But the clerk will never rent out a horror film to kids."

"I've already figured that out. I took Dad's video card from his dresser drawer. I'll tell the clerk that my father sent me down to rent the video for him."

"But...Gran won't let us watch it either. No way!"

Grrr! Patience, Maddie. That's what I told myself. Then I explained the second part of my plan to Alexander.

"We'll watch it after Gran goes to bed. If she stays up late tonight, we'll watch it tomorrow night. But if we're going to rent it for the whole weekend, I'll need your money. DO YOU UNDERSTAND?"

"Yes, but—"

Here I lost my patience and I told Alexander exactly what I thought.

"You're just a wimp. You'll never know a thing about violence! And you'll look like a total nerd at school on Monday."

Alexander immediately took out his money and gave it to me. I went into the video store.

Five minutes later I walked out with the video of *The Exterminator*.

Alexander couldn't believe it. I could hardly believe it myself. You know what happened?

I told my little story to the

clerk and he just said, "Don't waste your breath, kid. I've seen a thousand little liars like you before."

He knew exactly what I was doing, but he rented this unbelievably violent film to me anyway. It's amazing.

Honestly, some people have absolutely no conscience!

3
Very Scary

It was midnight.

Only Gran's snores disturbed the deathly silence, as Alexander and I tiptoed down into the bowels of the house.

The basement was as dark as a cave. I switched on my flashlight. Alexander slipped the videocassette into the VCR and pressed the PLAY button.

Terrifying music blared out. The title burst on to the screen in letters dripping with blood: *The Exterminator*.

Then a blood-curdling voice said, "POOR little creatures.

You POOR humans. I shall exterminate you all. HA! HA! HA!"

The Exterminator appeared. He was horrifying. He came up to a crowd of people. They all ran away. He stretched out his neck and his head got bigger and bigger. His eyes popped out of his sockets and he stared at us.

Alexander and I moved a little closer together. And even closer when the Exterminator said, "You can run, but you can't hide. I will catch you. HA! HA! HA!"

The Exterminator grabbed a girl about my age and crushed her in his hands. All the blood ran out of her body.

Her mother went mad with

grief and threw herself on the Exterminator. He picked up his gun and sliced her up, drooling with pleasure, "A family sandwich! Yum yum! HA! HA! HA!"

"Whew! This is kind of ... don't you think so?"

Alexander didn't answer. He was motionless, his mouth hanging open. He scared me.

Especially when I h-h-heard a noise behind me. Boy, was I scared! I yelled out:

— ...

I wanted to say, "Alexander, stop acting like an idiot! Say something, talk to me!" But not a sound came out of my mouth.

The noise came closer. On the screen the Exterminator was ripping someone's eyes out.

"YOU'LL BE SORRY! You're watching *The Exterminator* without me, you double-dealing traitors! That's not very nice."

It was Julian! GRRR! HE'LL be sorry, for scaring us like that! Alexander and I leaped up and started yelling at him, till he began to cry.

"You're mean! You never want to do anything with me. But I'm going to watch *The Exterminator* with you anyway."

We tried to explain to Julian that he was too young, but he didn't listen. We ordered him to go back to bed, and he left, muttering, "You'll be sorry."

Pretty soon he returned with Gran. At that very moment the Exterminator just happened to be mashing a poor old lady into mush, while chortling "HA! HA! HA! HA! H—"

Gran just cut him right off, in the middle of his laugh. And you know what? It was as if she had beaten the Exterminator, and I began to feel incredibly happy.

"It's time for you all to go to bed," said Gran, in a comforting voice.

Alexander, Julian, and I headed off in a line, like three naughty little ducklings. We weren't afraid going up the stairs, because Gran had turned on every single light in the house. And also because we knew that Gran was stronger than the Exterminator.

4
A Talk with Gran

Gran was fixing breakfast in silence. I had the feeling she was very angry. She's bound to punish us, I thought.

After breakfast she put Angel-baby in her stroller, picked up her umbrella, and announced, "We're going down to Garcia's corner store."

I figured that Gran was actually going to take us to the video store. It would be horrible. The closer we got, the angrier Gran seemed to get. But when we went into the video store, I realized that it wasn't us she was angry at.

She headed straight for the counter, right past the other customers, and started yelling at the clerk. I couldn't understand everything she said, but it was an earful.

"...shameless ...You are a monster! ... filth... unbridled violence ... contact the police!"

The clerk tried to calm Gran down.

"Hey, hold on, old lady. I've done nothing wrong."

I don't think he managed to convince Gran, because she gave him a rap on the knuckles with her umbrella.

"Then I'm doing nothing wrong either!" and she banged her umbrella down on *The Exterminator* cassette.

"Right?" she cried, waving her umbrella around. "The old lady is doing nothing wrong. You agree?"

The clerk was so terrified that he decided to call the police himself.

"Let's go, children, " said Gran. "I find the smell in this establishment disagreeable."

As usual, Julian was totally out of it.

"Of course it smells bad, Gran. It's full of stinking bombs."

Gran thought Julian was extremely witty and she burst out laughing. Did she ever laugh! She laughed so hard that we started giggling, too. Then everyone in the store started laughing.

Everyone except the clerk, who was holding his head in his hands, as if Gran had bopped him with the umbrella too.

The rest of the day was happy and fun. Gran didn't scold us at all. She didn't even mention *The Exterminator* again. Kind of weird...

At bedtime, I said to myself that Alexander and I were lucky that the whole thing had turned out so well.

Well, it didn't turn out so well in my dreams. I dreamed that the Exterminator was chasing me. He came closer, I could feel his hands on my neck, he is going to mash me to a pulp ... *Gran*!

I ran to Gran's bedroom to escape from the Exterminator.

My heart was beating so fast it scared me. Even my shadow on the wall scared me. Everything scared me.

As I ran I thought that my mother was right: now I was MARKED FOR LIFE.

"Well, it all depends on you," said Gran, as I snuggled into her

arms. "If you don't want to have any more nightmares, you have to let the Exterminator sleep."

"Let the Exterminator sleep? I don't understand."

"When you let him out of the video, it's as if you woke him up," Gran explained. "It's as if you made him come alive. And the longer you let him be alive, the stronger he'll get. Then he can take over your life."

"But Gran, that means that piles of people's lives are in danger. And I can never watch a horror movie again. That doesn't make sense."

My Gran is amazing! Do you know what she asked me?

"Would you like to watch *The Exterminator* again tomorrow, or the day after?"

"Uh...no."

"That's what I thought. You would rather wait a bit. A month, maybe a year. And the longer you wait, the more the Exterminator will shrink, in your mind. And he won't seem as scary to you. To me, he was absolutely ridiculous."

That's what I like about Gran. You can talk to her. And then she lets you decide for yourself.

Since I wanted to get back to sleep, I thought I would let the Exterminator sleep too, in his videocassette. And I wouldn't be in a hurry to wake him up. It will be quite a while before I think he's absolutely ridiculous. Whew!

5
A Triumph for Maddie, but...

The next day, Alexander really did look sick. In the schoolbus he didn't say a word. He was as white as a sheet, as if he had had no sleep.

"No, I did sleep," he told me, "and that's the problem. I had nightmares all night long."

"Poor Alexander. You shouldn't have watched *The Exterminator*. You're too sensitive for that kind of movie. But don't tell anyone at school that you had nightmares; they'll just laugh at you."

At school, no one mentioned

having any nightmares, of course. But no one mentioned the Exterminator either. Even the leader of our gang, Patrick Walsh, didn't have anything to say about it.

Usually he goes on and on about everything he's done, and buries us in swear words and insults. He makes us feel so small. That's why he's the leader.

Well, I thought there was something funny about his silence. So I asked him casually, "What did you do on Friday night?"

"Uh ... I ... uh ..."

This was getting fishier and fishier. I began to think he hadn't watched *The Exterminator*. That gave me the nerve to poke a little fun at him.

"So that's what you did Friday, you did 'uh'..."

The whole gang burst out laughing. I couldn't get over it. Patrick Walsh said nothing. For the first time, he was the one who felt squashed. Wow! I'd been waiting for this moment for a long time.

"Well, *I* watched *The Exterminator*."

"I don't believe you," Patrick Walsh finally said.

"Ask Alexander!"

"It's t-t-true, she did. We weren't going to miss such a good movie for all the chips in the world." Alexander sounded more confident than I expected.

Well, I can tell you that the others were really impressed.

Do you know why? Because no one else had been allowed to watch the movie! I told them straight out what I thought of them.

"You're all a bunch of wimps. If you're going to ask permission for every little thing you want to do, well, you won't get very far."

I told them how I had tricked the clerk at the video store AND my grandmother.

Alexander and I instantly became stars. We were bombarded with questions.

"The story? Well, there isn't really any story. The Exterminator exterminates people, that's all. Is it really bloody? Yeah, it is, but it's not as bad as all that."

"Weren't you scared?"

"A bit, at the beginning, but you get used to the violence, don't you, Alexander?"

"Yeah, oh yes...yeah, you get used to it. Even if you have a nightmare, who cares, right?"

GRRR! I knew that Alexander would put his foot in his mouth. Patrick Walsh would laugh his head off.

But no, Walsh didn't say a word. No one was paying any attention to him. It was as if he didn't exist. He had become transparent.

But then, wouldn't you know it, Clementine, the biggest brain in the class, piped up with the trick question. You know what she asked, in her little mousey voice?

"How does the movie end?"

Alexander looked over at me in a panic. I felt like I was taking a test I hadn't studied for. If I couldn't answer this question, I would be TOAST for the rest of the year. They would tease me unmercifully. I would look ridiculous. RIDICULOUS. But that gave me an idea.

"We don't know how the movie ends," I said, "because we didn't watch it till the end."

"Yeah, we never watched the end," Alexander supported me. "It's the honest truth. How come? I don't—"

I interrupted Alexander before he could stick his foot in his mouth again.

"Because not only was the Exterminator not the least bit scary, we thought he was boring. We thought he was RIDICULOUS. Didn't we, Alexander?"

"Ridiculous? Yeah, that's right, we thought he was RIDICULOUS."

"RIDICULOUS? Really? You thought he was ridiculous, did you?"

Oh, right, there was Walsh talking in his tough voice. The poor guy, he couldn't scare anyone anymore. I turned around to put him in his place, and then I got a TERRIBLE shock.

There was THE EXTERMINATOR in person. Deep down inside, I cried out "Gran!"

6
Maddie versus the Exterminator

In the schoolbus on the way home, I was the one who was silent. I must have looked as sick as Alexander did this morning.

My stomach hurt and my heart ached. My arms were all bruised. Even before the Exterminator crushed me in his hands, I had already turned to mush.

What happened was awful.

The Exterminator asked who was the leader of the gang. No one answered. Everyone lost their voice. So the Exterminator turned on the smallest one in the group, Clementine.

"If you don't tell me, I'll tear your skin off and draw and quarter you."

The little mouse had turned into a scared, cornered little mouse. It made me sick to see how terrified she was. But she still managed to point to Patrick Walsh, who yelled, "I'm not the leader! She is—Maddie!"

I don't know whether the others agreed with him, because no one else said a word. Any other time, I would have been happy to be chosen leader. But now it was the last thing I wanted.

The Exterminator couldn't have cared less. He grabbed my arm and dug his nails in. With

the other hand he made a sharp movement.

SSSSLINNNGGG!

The blade of a knife appeared before my eyes. Through my tears I could see it glinting horribly.

"Take up a collection," the Exterminator ordered. "I want fifty dollars, tomorrow, at four o'clock, by the pond in the park. And don't say a word to anyone, or else—SLASH! I'll—"

The Exterminator laughed a bloodthirsty laugh. Then he disappeared.

I began to feel sick. And I felt even sicker when I found I could only collect $6.34.

I didn't know what to do. If I don't bring the money, the Exterminator will ... I guess he'll kill me. And if I tell anyone, SLASH! Same thing.

I had never felt so alone. It was too awful. When I got home, I ran straight to Gran and told her everything.

"Maddie, there is no Exterminator. He does not exist. Do you understand?"

"Maybe he doesn't exist, but then there's a fake Exterminator who's just as horrible as the real one. And he does exist."

"Well, yes, but that's the point. He's a fake. If he was really so horrible, he wouldn't need to disguise himself in order to scare you. I bet he was just as scared as you were."

"Scared? What would he be scared of?"

"Of being found out!" Gran

added, mysteriously, "And that is exactly what we are going to do."

I was absolutely positive that Gran was stronger than the Exterminator.

* * * *

At school the next day all the gang members were looking sick. Nobody had slept the night before. They were all worried about me.

"Don't worry," I reassured them all mysteriously. "I have a plan."

I would have liked to explain to them what my plan was, but as it was Gran's plan, I didn't know what to tell them.

All she had said was that Alexander and I should go straight to the park after school, so we would be there before the Exterminator.

At 3:30, we ran to the park, behind the little stand near the pond. Gran was already there with Julian and Angelbaby. She had her umbrella too.

From our little shelter we could see all around us without being seen. Time passed. Julian still had no idea what was going on.

"Why did we come to the park if we're not going to play?" he asked.

"We're playing Exterminator," said Gran. "Shhh! Look, here he comes."

"Is that the Exterminator?" wondered Julian. "I think it must be Son of Exterminator, because he's kind of little."

"Julian caught on right away," said Gran. "Your Exterminator is just a little rascal who needs to be taught a good lesson. Give him the money," she told me, handing me an envelope. "Then we'll come up and catch him red-handed. Don't be afraid."

I wasn't afraid. I was furious—furious at myself.

To think that Julian caught on right away! And I had stood there quaking before this twerp.

He jumped when he saw me. "Aaaah!"

I saw the terrible knife of the Exterminator. It was made of rubber.

I gave him the money anyway. The twerp couldn't get over how easy it was, and he didn't even try to intimidate me.

"Ha! Ha! Ha! H—"

This time I cut him off in the middle of his bloodthirsty laugh.

"You're trapped!"

The fake Exterminator turned around and saw the others. He tried to run away, but he tripped over Gran's umbrella and fell into the pond. SPLASH!

When he dragged himself out of the water, he looked even smaller. He looked RIDICU-LOUS, with a big lily pad draped over his head. When he tried to pull it off, his mask came off too.

"NICHOLAS GARCIA!"

Son of Exterminator was none other than the son of the owners of the corner store! And he was shaking in fear, and shivering like a wet hen.

Gran took off her raincoat and put it around Nicholas's shoulders, saying, "Let's go home now. We don't want the Exterminator to catch a cold."

I didn't think it was funny at all. Boy, I'm going to get even with Nicholas Garcia somehow!

7
Maddie, Leader of the Gang

Nicholas Garcia wouldn't crack, no matter how much I threatened him.

"I'll tell your dad you steal chips from his store. I thought you were my friend. You give me chips and then you—"

"Hey!" yelled Alexander. "You gave stolen chips to Maddie and not to me? How come?"

"We will make you talk," said Julian, "you cringing cad, you joking jackanapes, you stinking stink bomb!"

"Children, that's enough," Gran stepped in. "You won't get

anything out of Nicholas with threats. I think he has already been terrorized enough."

"YES! I AM being terrorized!" cried Nicholas.

Gran motioned us to be quiet. She comforted Nicholas. Without asking him a single question, she got him to talk to her.

Nicholas had been threatened with a real knife. Not by a fake Exterminator, but by a gang of real hoodlums. He had to give them $50 tomorrow, or else... SLASH!

"They told me to take the money out of the cash register at the store. But that's impossible. My dad is always there. That's why...I had to, or else the gang of... will—" sobbed Nicholas.

"The gang isn't going to do anything to you," said Gran. "I'll take care of them. What gang is it?"

"The Bald Eagles," muttered Nicholas, as if he was afraid of being heard.

"The Bald Eagles!" I cried. "I know them, I already ran into them. They're hoodlums. They're very violent. You don't want to fool around with them."

Even Gran didn't think the Bald Eagles were ridiculous. This time she called the police. And a lot of other people.

* * * *

The next day our basement was full of people. All our friends were there, and their parents, too. And our teachers. Even one of the police officers who arrested the Bald Eagles.

First Gran explained what had happened. Then everyone discussed it. We wanted to prevent anything like that from happening again. After a moment, Nicholas asked if he could speak.

"I would like to say that ... I think Maddie did the right thing ... what you should do if you're threatened. She wasn't afraid to tell someone. And she rescued me."

I couldn't get over it. I said to myself, "The only reason I told someone was because I was so scared!"

I didn't say anything out loud. And I think that was the right thing to do. Because Nicholas suggested that I should be made the leader of the gang, for having displayed such courage.

Everyone applauded. Even Patrick Walsh. Wow! When it was quiet again, I was about to say that I would accept this great honour, but the REAL leader was Gran. But then I heard a suspicious noise coming from above... Someone was coming down the stairs.

"Hi! We're home! We missed you!"

It was my parents! They came home earlier than planned. When they saw all the people, they stopped short, their mouths agape, as if they were watching a horror movie.

Julian explained what was going on. "Maddie wasn't afraid of the Exterminator. So Gran made the stinker fall in the pond, and his mask came off.

He's the boy from the corner store, and he had to give money to the Bald Eagles. And you don't fool around with them, or else SLASH! And now we're all talking about it!"

My parents didn't understand right away. Then they understood quite clearly that I had rented *The Exterminator*.

I suddenly got the feeling that

everything wasn't going to turn out as well as I hoped. There would be punishment and it would be as bad as anything the Exterminator could dish out.

Anyway, I plan to explain to my parents that I am already marked for life. I know I will never get used to violence, especially real violence.

So maybe they won't punish me.

Look for these First Novels!
Collect the entire series!

About Maddie
   Maddie in Danger
   Maddie Goes to Paris
   Maddie Wants Music
   That's Enough, Maddie
   Maddie in Goal

About Mooch
   Mooch Forever
   Hang On, Mooch
   Mooch Gets Jealous
   Mooch and Me

About Arthur
   Arthur's Problem Puppy
   Arthur's Dad
   Arthur Throws a Tantrum

About the Swank twins
   The Swank Prank
   Swank Talk

About Mikey Mite
   Mikey Mite Goes to School
   Mikey Mite's Big Problem

About the Loonies
   Loonie Summer
   The Loonies Arrive

And meet Fred and Raphael!
   Fred's Dream Cat
   Video Rivals

And more to come!

For more information about these and other fine books for young readers contact

   Formac Publishing Company Limited
   5502 Atlantic Street
   Halifax, Nova Scotia B3H 1G4
   (902) 421-7022 Fax (902) 425-0166